This **Little Tiger** book belongs to:

_____

_____

_____

For my mum
~ D B
For Andy, Caroline,
Charlotte and Harry
~ T W

LITTLE TIGER PRESS

An imprint of Magi Publications

1 The Coda Centre, 189 Munster Road, London SW6 6AW

www.littletigerpress.com

First published in Great Britain 2005
This edition published 2007

Text copyright © David Bedford 2005
Illustrations copyright © Tim Warnes 2005
David Bedford and Tim Warnes have asserted their rights
to be identified as the author and illustrator of this work
under the Copyright, Designs and Patents Act, 1988.

A CIP catalogue record for this book is available
from the British Library.

Printed in China

2 4 6 8 10 9 7 5 3 1

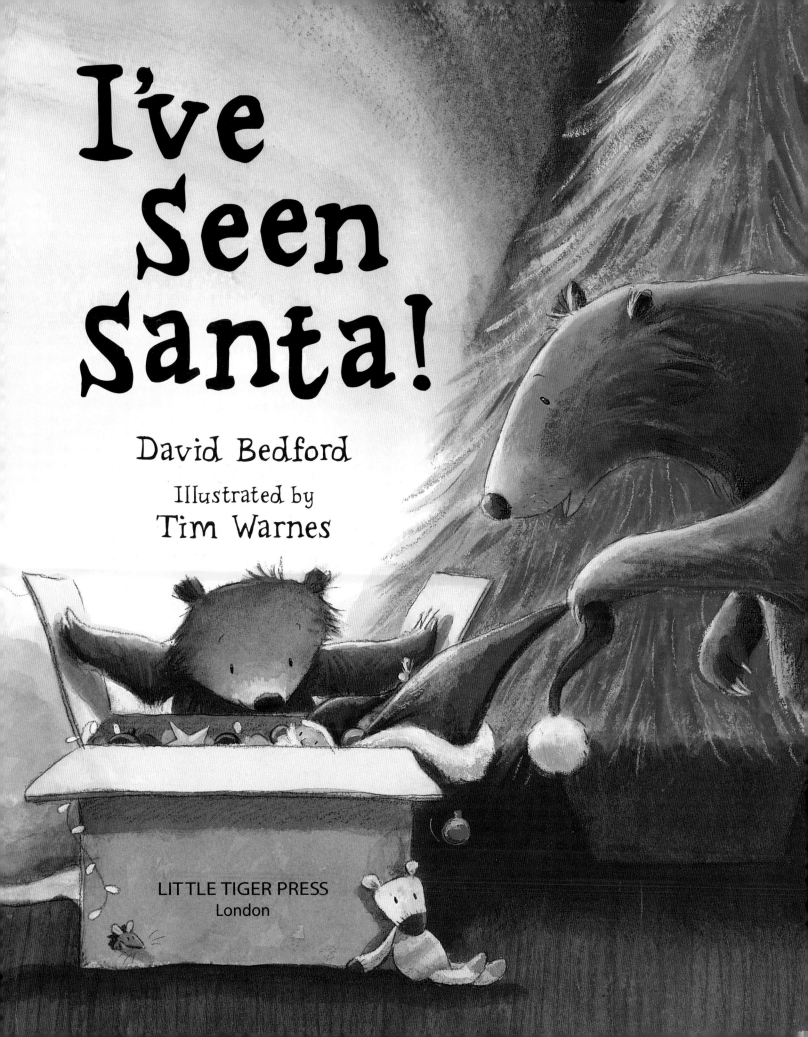

I've Seen Santa!

David Bedford

Illustrated by
Tim Warnes

LITTLE TIGER PRESS
London

It was Christmas Eve and Little Bear was looking forward to seeing Santa.

"Is Santa as big as you?" he asked Big Bear

"Nearly," said Big Bear, proudly.

"Oh," said Little Bear, looking worried.
"Will Santa fit down our chimney, then?"
    "Of course he will!" said Big Bear. "I'll show you."
    Big Bear went outside and climbed into
the chimney . . .

CRASH!

"See?" said Big Bear, from a cloud of soot.
"Santa will get in, no problem!"

"Santa won't come if he sees this mess!"
said Mummy Bear.
"We'll help clean up," said Little Bear.

"Does Santa visit bears
all over the world?"
said Little Bear.
"Yes," said Big Bear.
"He goes to every
house."

"Hmm," said Little Bear. "He might not have time to come here, and then I won't have any presents."
"Don't worry," said Mummy Bear. "Santa will come just as soon as you go to sleep."

For SANTA
(paws off,
Big Bear)

Little Bear didn't want to go to sleep.
He wanted to see Santa. He listened to
Mummy Bear and Big Bear going to bed.
And then . . . GLUG, GLUG, GLUG, GLUG!

What was that noise?
Someone was downstairs!

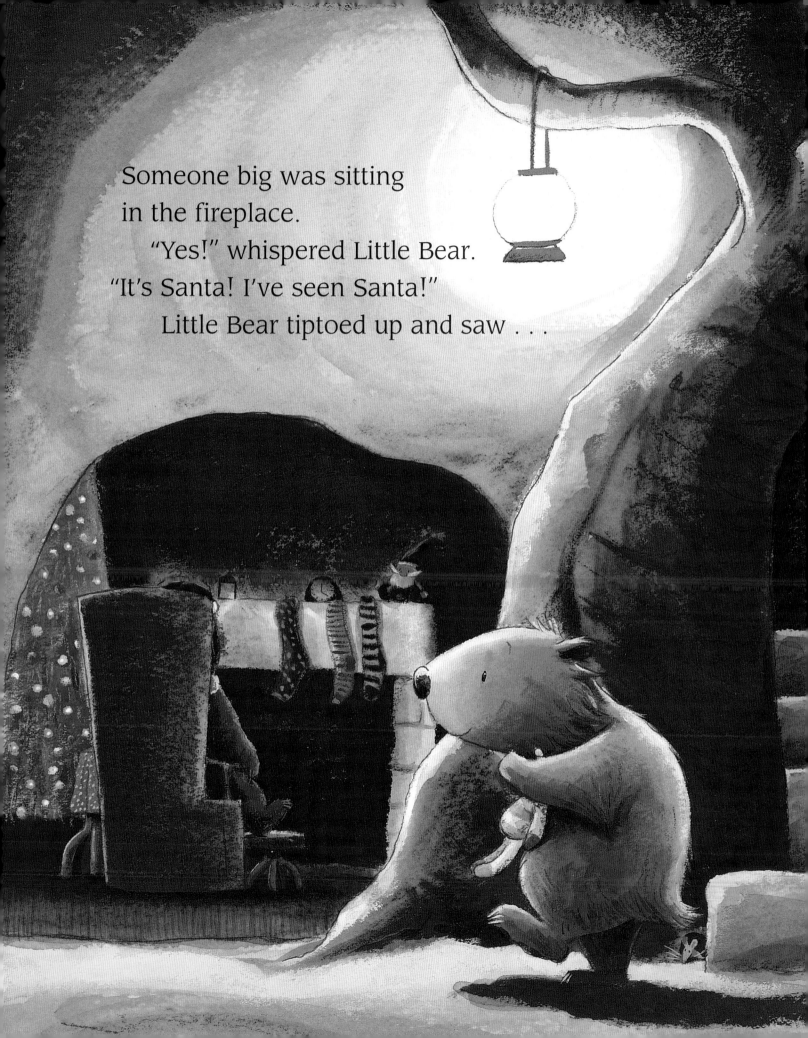

Someone big was sitting
in the fireplace.
"Yes!" whispered Little Bear.
"It's Santa! I've seen Santa!"
Little Bear tiptoed up and saw . . .

. . . Big Bear!

"That's Santa's milk!" said Little Bear.
"I only wanted a sip," said Big Bear,
"before I go to sleep." He took Little
Bear's hand. "Come on, Little Bear.
Let's go to bed."

Little Bear tried to stay awake, but he
soon fell into a doze.

Then a loud noise downstairs woke
him up.

MUNCH! MUNCH! MUNCH! MUNCH!

Someone big was
standing by the
Christmas tree.
This time it had to be . . .

. . . Big Bear again!

"You're eating Santa's mince
pies now!" said Little Bear.
      "I was hungry," said Big Bear.

"If Santa's as greedy as you,"
said Mummy Bear, coming
downstairs, "he'll be too big
and he WILL get stuck in the
chimney! Now go to bed
and go to sleep –
both of you!"

Little Bear went to bed, but he couldn't go to sleep. He was too worried. He woke up Big Bear to ask him a question.

"What if Santa eats too many mince pies and then gets stuck in the chimney?" he whispered.

"Hmm," said Big Bear.
"Let's keep watch to make sure he's OK," said Little Bear. "We can hide so he won't see us."

"Shhh!" whispered Little Bear
from their hiding place.
"I can hear something!
It MUST be Santa this time!"

Someone was putting
presents in their stockings!
Big Bear turned on his
torch to see . . .

. . . Mummy Bear!

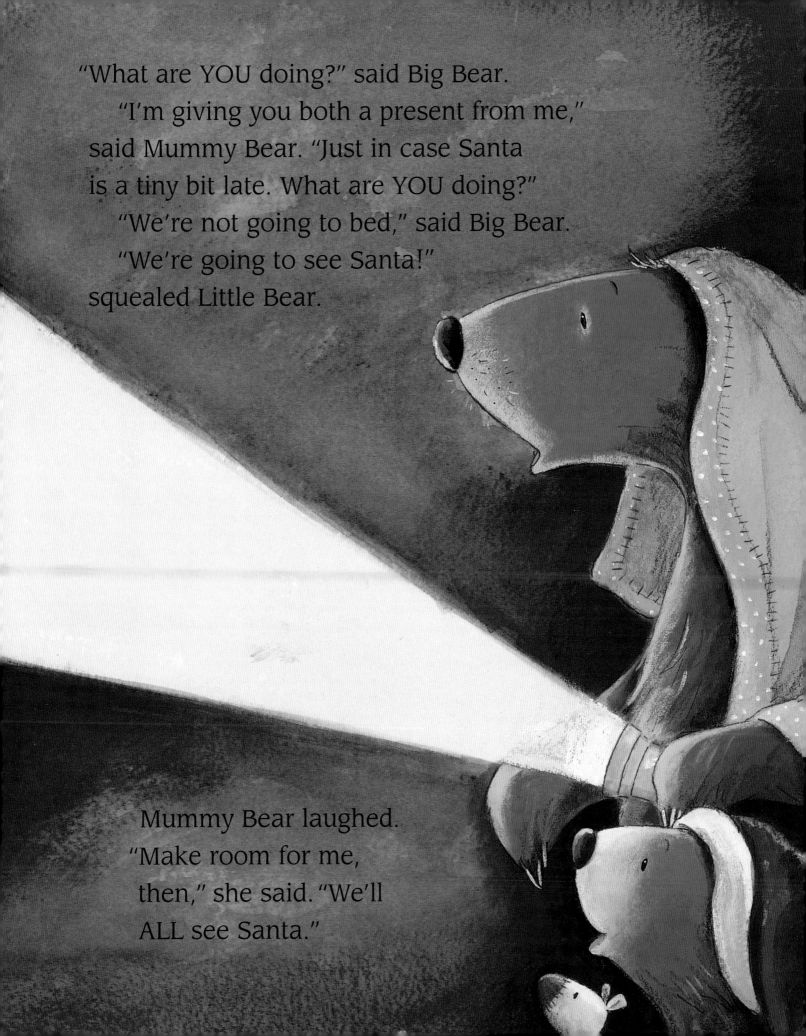

"What are YOU doing?" said Big Bear.
     "I'm giving you both a present from me,"
said Mummy Bear. "Just in case Santa
is a tiny bit late. What are YOU doing?"
     "We're not going to bed," said Big Bear.
     "We're going to see Santa!"
squealed Little Bear.

     Mummy Bear laughed.
     "Make room for me,
     then," she said. "We'll
     ALL see Santa."

Little Bear, Big Bear and
Mummy Bear stayed downstairs
all through the night.

But they never did see Santa . . .

. . . even though
Santa saw them!

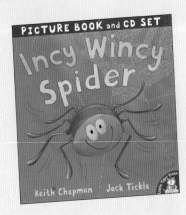
PICTURE BOOK and CD SET
Incy Wincy Spider
Keith Chapman · Jack Tickle

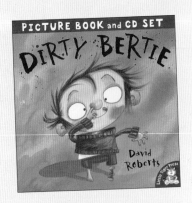
PICTURE BOOK and CD SET
DiRTY BERTiE
David Roberts

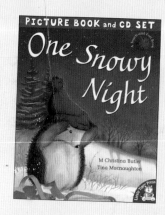
PICTURE BOOK and CD SET
One Snowy Night
M Christina Butler
Tina Macnaughton

Perfect presents from Little Tiger Tales!

PICTURE BOOK and CD SET
Laura's Star
Klaus Baumgart

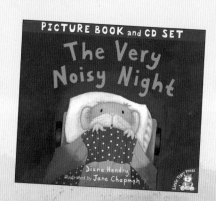
PICTURE BOOK and CD SET
The Very Noisy Night
Diana Hendry
Illustrated by Jane Chapman

PICTURE BOOK and CD SET
I don't want to go to bed!
Julie Sykes · Tim Warnes

For information regarding any other Little Tiger Tales
Picture Book and CD sets or for our catalogue, please contact us:
Little Tiger Press, 1 The Coda Centre, 189 Munster Road, London SW6 6AW
Tel: 020 7385 6333 Fax: 020 7385 7333 E-mail: info@littletiger.co.uk www.littletigerpress.com